For Rey – the original Pipsqueak

R.M.

For Ivor, who is cuddly but hates cuddles
S.W.

WALKER BOOKS
AND SUBSIDIARIES
LONDON · BOSTON · SYDNEY · AUCKLAND

First published 2022 by Walker Books Ltd, 87 Vauxhall Walk, London SE11 5HJ • This edition published 2023 • Text © 2022 Ross Montgomery • Illustrations © 2022 Sarah Warburton
The right of Ross Montgomery and Sarah Warburton to be identified as author and illustrator respectively of this work has been asserted in accordance with the Copyright, Designs
and Patents Act 1988 • This book has been typeset in Intro • Printed in China • All rights reserved. No part of this book may be reproduced, transmitted or stored in an information
retrieval system in any form or by any means, graphic, electronic or mechanical, including photocopying, taping and recording, without prior written permission from the publisher.
British Library Cataloguing in Publication Data: a catalogue record for this book is available from the British Library • ISBN 978-1-5295-1283-0 • www.walker.co.uk • 10 9 8 7 6 5 4 3 2 1

This Walker book
belongs to:

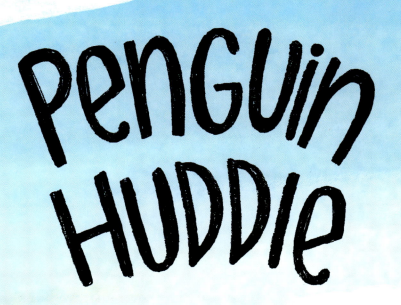

PENGUIN HUDDLE

Ross Montgomery   Sarah Warburton

The penguin pack played all day long on the frozen southern pole.
Some went ice skating...

Some went fishing...

The others juggled snowballs!

And when the sun went down,

and stars filled the cold, dark sky...

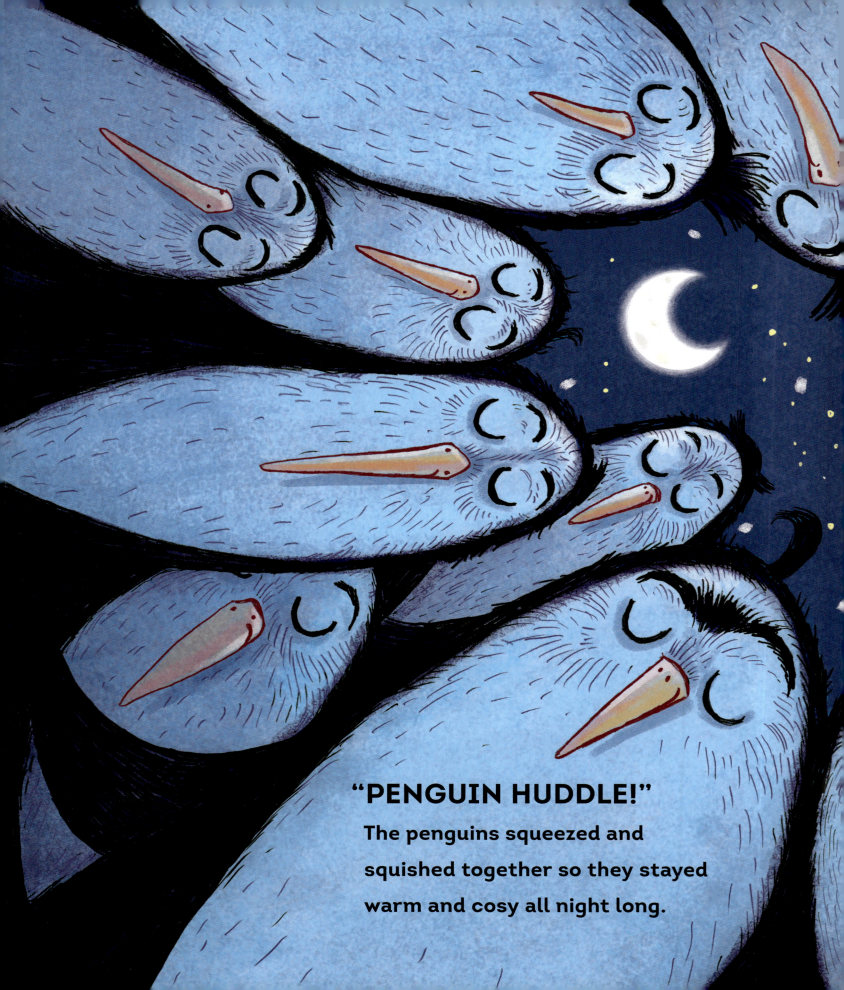

"PENGUIN HUDDLE!"
The penguins squeezed and
squished together so they stayed
warm and cosy all night long.

But one night, there was a gale that blew as hard as a herd of mammoths and froze the wind to the mountain.

When the penguins woke up

the next morning,

they

were
stuck!

The penguins pulled and puffed and shuffled and scuffled,
but it was no use. They were frozen together,
like a giant penguin ice pop!

From the middle of the huddle came a tiny voice.
"Let's ask our friends to help!" said Pipsqueak,
the smallest of them all.

The snow hares heaved
and huffed,

and the walruses prised and puffed,

but they didn't budge one bit.

What a penguin muddle!

"What will we do?" the penguins panicked.
"I've got an idea!" said Pipsqueak, and he pointed
to a place far, far away...

The penguins set off across the great and gleaming ocean.

They travelled by Iceberg Express ...

Albatross Airways ...

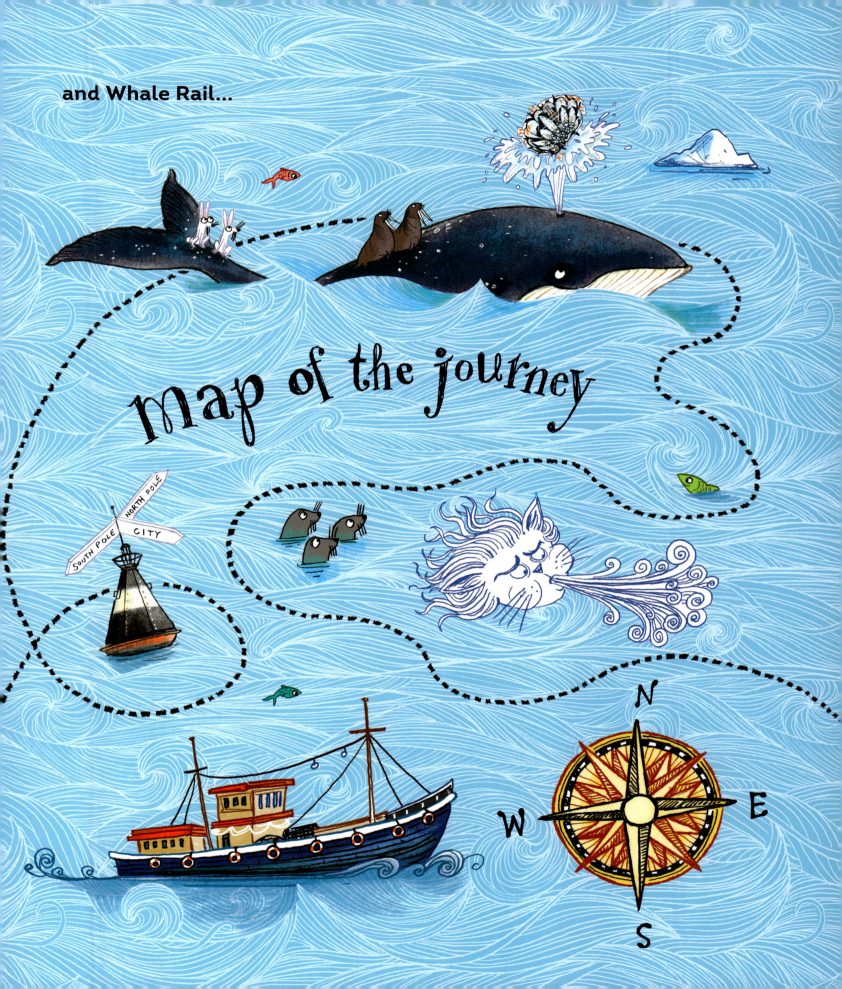

Until finally, they came to a shining city.

"There's got to be someone who can help us here," said Pipsqueak.

The streets were filled with thousands of different animals from all over the world. The penguins searched high and low for someone who could lend a paw, hoof or flipper.

But ... the baker's warm doughnuts didn't defrost them,

the barber's sharp claws couldn't crack them,

and the beetles' bowling balls bounced right off them.

What a penguin struggle!

Just when the penguins were feeling lumpier
and grumpier than ever and ready to give up,
Pipsqueak had another idea.

"Look at the poster, everyone!
We can ask the Doctopus for help."

The penguins pulled and puffed and shuffled and scuffled as fast as they could, but they were still too slow.

"We'll never get there before it closes!" they said.

"Never fear!" said their new animal friends...

"We'll get you there!"
The penguins raced through the city streets to get to the Doctopus in time.

Nee-naw! Nee-naw! Nee-naw!

The Doctopus was about to leave his office when the penguin pack pushed in.

"You have to help us, Doc," the penguins cried. "We're frozen stiff!"

The Doctopus listened with a little smile as they told their story. "Bless my tentacles!" he said. "I think you've solved this penguin puzzle on your own. The answer is right at your feet!"

The penguins couldn't believe their eyes.
After all their adventures, their penguin huddle
had melted into a penguin puddle!

"We're free! Yippee!" they sang.

But when the dancing was done, poor Pipsqueak
wasn't happy any more. "I loved our penguin huddle.
We were squished and squeezed and lumpy and grumpy,
but we were close, too. And now it's gone, I miss it."

They made a penguin promise.

"Whenever the night is cold," said one,
"we'll always be here to keep you safe and warm."

"Wherever you go," said another,
"you will always have friends who can help you."

"We might not have our penguin huddle,
  but you can always have ...

a penguin cuddle."

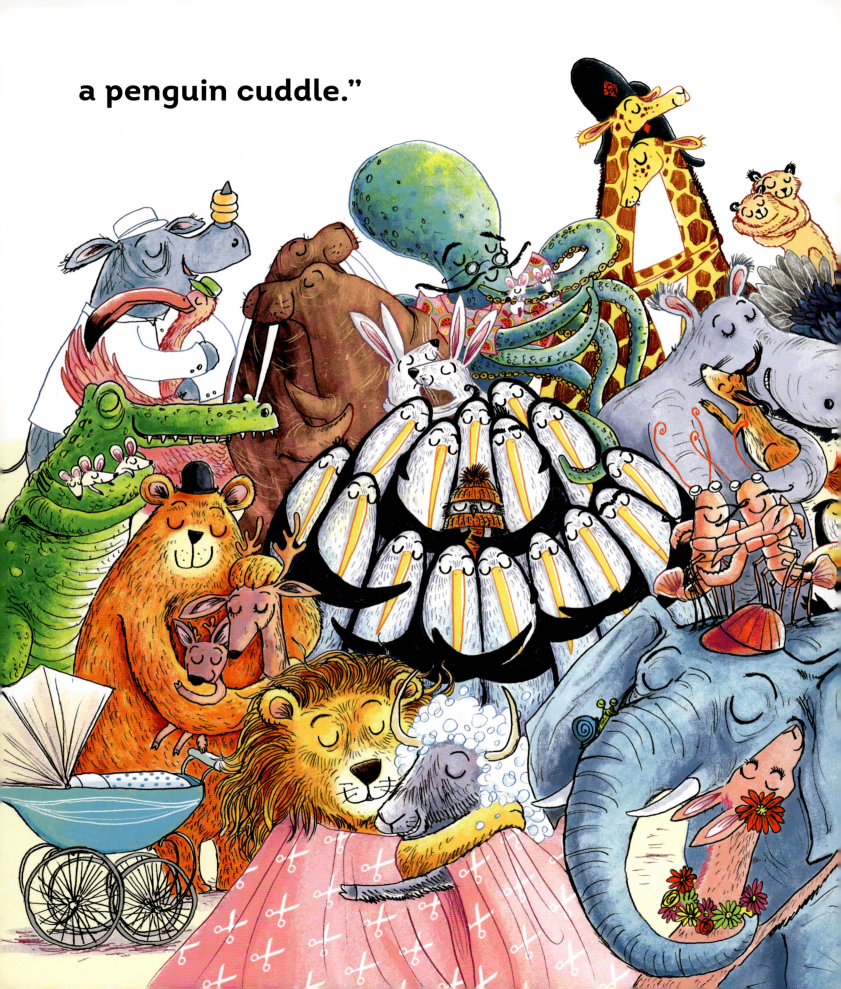

Huddle up with another story from Ross Montgomery and Sarah Warburton

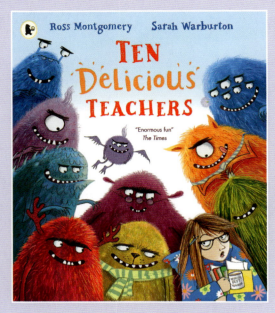

ISBN: 978-1-5295-0417-0

Shortlisted for the Laugh Out Loud Book Awards 2023
Highly Commended in the Teach Early Years Award 2022
Winner of the Bishop's Stortford Picture Book Award 2022

"A playfully wicked back-to-school alternative."
The Bookseller

"A great way to learn numbers while laughing out loud."
The Daily Mail & The Scottish Daily Mail

"Funny and irreverent. It's easy to imagine this one being a huge hit at school story time."
The Guardian

"A comic countdown chant. Great fun to read aloud."
The Times

Available from all good booksellers   www.walker.co.uk